Forget✿Me✿Not
Beautiful Buttercup

MICHAEL
BROAD

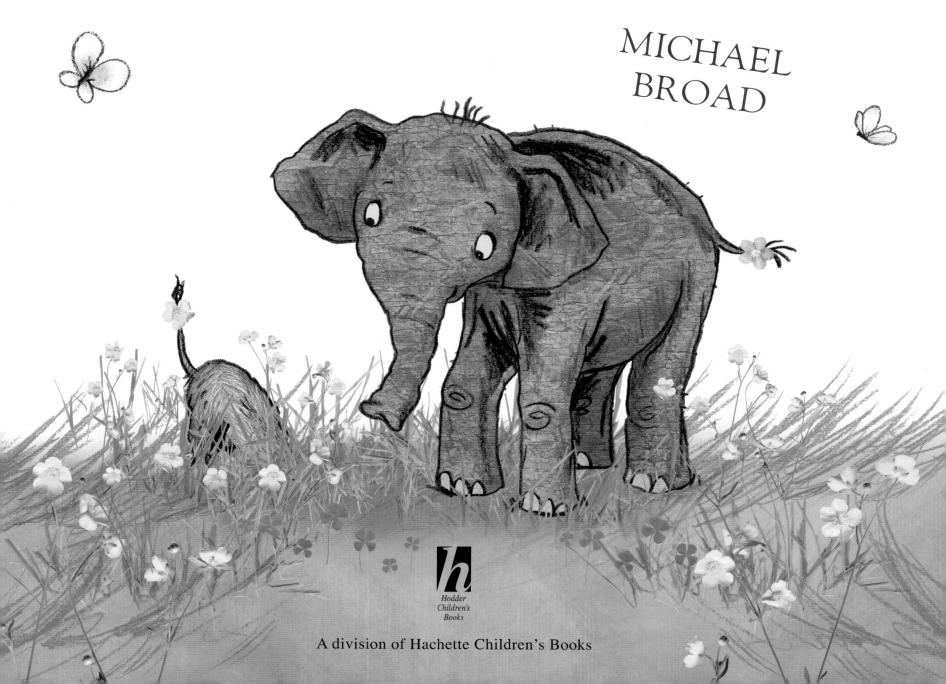

Hodder
Children's
Books

A division of Hachette Children's Books

SEARCHING FOR LUSH GREEN PASTURES, the herd joined the other animals moving towards the distant mountains. Everyone was tired and hungry.

For Antony.

First published in 2011
by Hodder Children's Books

Text and illustrations copyright © Michael Broad 2011

Hodder Children's Books
338 Euston Road
London NW1 3BH

Hodder Children's Books Australia
Level 17/207 Kent Street
Sydney NSW 2000

A catalogue record of this book is available from the British Library.

ISBN: 978 0 340 99943 1
10 9 8 7 6 5 4 3 2 1

Printed in China

Hodder Children's Books is a division
of Hachette Children's Books.
An Hachette UK Company
www.hachette.co.uk

Can you spot the green lizard?

Only one young elephant was keen to make new friends.

'Can I go and play, Mama?' asked Forget-Me-Not, seeing some warthogs having fun.
'Yes, my darling,' smiled his mother. 'But play nicely with the little ones.'

'I will,' he promised and hurried over to join them.

But not all of the warthogs were having fun. The littlest one looked very sad indeed.

Her brothers were calling her names.

'Big snout,' snorted one.

'Scruffy bristles,' sniffed another.

'Teeny-tiny, ugly-wugly!'

they all jeered.

'My mama says to play nicely with the little ones,' said Forget-Me-Not bravely. 'And teasing someone small is not very nice at all.'

'Then **you** can play with her!'
grunted the warthogs
as they scampered away.

'I'm Forget-Me-Not,' said the young elephant, kindly.
'What's your name?'

'I'm Buttercup,' said the shy little warthog.
'But everyone calls me Ugly.'

'I don't think you're ugly,' said Forget-Me-Not
and he played with his new friend all day long.

The hyenas laughed at how little Buttercup was.
But Forget-Me-Not ignored them.

Being small meant that she was very good at playing hide-and-seek.

He took no notice of the reed frogs when they chuckled at Buttercup's long, scruffy bristles.

They were just right for tickling his trunk,
which always made him giggle.

And when the ostriches squawked at Buttercup's big snout, she used it to nudge a ball between their spindly legs.

Then Forget-Me-Not chased after her, which made the ostriches squawk even louder!

'Everyone is unkind to Buttercup because of the way she looks,' said Forget-Me-Not as he cuddled next to his mama that evening. 'But I think she's beautiful.'

'That's because you see what's
on the inside,' said his mother.
'One day, the others will see it, too.'

'And then they'll know how
special she is?' asked Forget-Me-Not,
hopefully.

'With a friend like you,
I'm certain they will,' she said and
stroked the little elephant's head
until he fell fast asleep.

The following day, the animals reached
the mountains. But no one knew which
path led to the lush green pastures.

The hyenas were silent.
The reed frogs hid beneath their parasols.
And the ostriches buried their heads
in the sand.

'I think I can help,' said Buttercup and she whispered into Forget-Me-Not's ear.

'Buttercup can find the way!' cried Forget-Me-Not.

'Ugly can't possibly help us,' scoffed the other animals.

But she did. Little Buttercup's big snout could smell the sweet grass and the scent of her favourite flowers. Her long bristles felt the slight cool breeze.

And she was small enough to stand on Forget-Me-Not's back and lead everyone through the mountains.

Soon the animals reached the lush green pastures full of bright yellow buttercups. They looked at the little warthog gratefully. She had wanted to help everyone even after they were mean to her.

And suddenly they saw what Forget-Me-Not had known all along. Buttercup was truly beautiful.